BURLINGAME PUBLIC LIBRARY
P9-DHI-474

To the river that brought me here—J. P.

For my parents, all four of them.
And for my wolf mothers Kuniko, Masako & Shihan—Z. A.

Library of Congress Cataloging-in-Publication Data available.

ISBN 978-1-4521-7715-1

Manufactured in China.

Design by Alice Seiler and Jill Turney.
Typeset in Mr Eaves Modern, Prater Block, and Bizzle-Chizzle.
The illustrations in this book were rendered in gouache,
colored pencil, and ink.

10 9 8 7 6 5 4 3 2 1

Chronicle Books LLC
680 Second Street
San Francisco, California 94107

Chronicle Books—we see things differently.
Become part of our community at www.chroniclekids.com.

OVER the MOON

By James Proimos

Illustrated by Zoey Abbott

chronicle books · san francisco

When a baby floats down a river,
she doesn’t think about her place in the world.

She just goes with the flow.

When two wolves sit on the river's edge,
the first wolf thinks about good and evil,
light and dark, right and wrong.

The second wolf thinks about dinner.

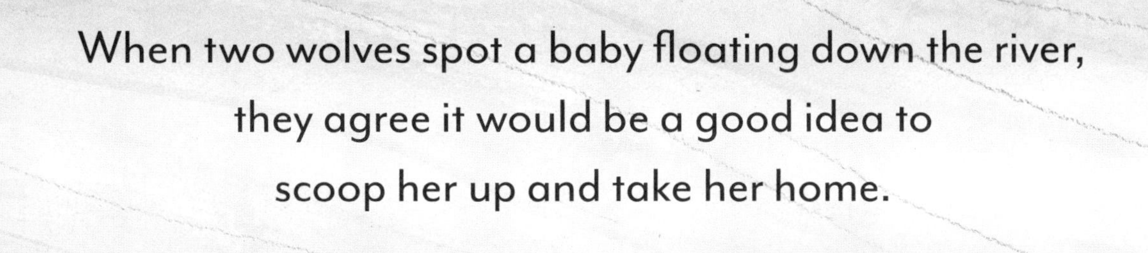

When two wolves spot a baby floating down the river, they agree it would be a good idea to scoop her up and take her home.

So they do.

When the two wolves get the baby home, they are both over the moon with joy.

The first wolf says, “We will nourish her and teach her about good and evil, dark and light, right and wrong.”

The second wolf says,

"I was planning on eating her."

But the wolves do teach her well . . .

and the baby grows into a young girl.

When the first wolf says, "I love you, child,"
and the second wolf says,
"I must admit you make a better girl
than you would have made a meal,"

the girl is happy.

The days pass, and the girl
grows stronger

and wiser.

The first wolf says,
"Time moves too fast."

The second wolf says,
"I'm afraid she will leave us one day."

"That was the whole point of nourishing her and teaching her about good and evil, dark and light, right and wrong," says the first wolf.

One day, when the girl goes out to pick berries for dinner she sees something she has never seen before.

She runs home.
She does not even know why.

When night falls the girl can't stop
thinking about what she saw.
The world is upside down.
She is not the girl she was before.

The girl goes back to the
spot again.

And again.

And again.

When the girl tells the wolves it is time for her to go, the first wolf says, "That is why we nourished you and taught you about good and evil, light and dark, right and wrong."

The second wolf tries hard not to, but sheds a tear.

Suddenly, the ground feels like a river,
and the current takes her to a building.

And to an open door.

Now, the girl and the wolves
will spend their days apart.

But when each day ends,
the wolves will be there to scoop
the girl into their arms
and take her home.

As they did from the river
so very long ago.

Rivers
of the
WORLD